MIKIS
AND THE
DONKEY

Written by
Bibi Dumon Tak
Illustrated by Philip Hopman
Translated by Laura Watkinson

Eerdmans Books for Young Readers
Grand Rapids, Michigan • Cambridge, U.K.

First published 2011 in Amsterdam, The Netherlands by
Em. Querido Uitgeverij B.V.

This edition published 2014 in the United States of America by
Eerdmans Books for Young Readers,
an imprint of Wm. B. Eerdmans Publishing Co.
2140 Oak Industrial Dr. NE, Grand Rapids, Michigan 49505
P.O. Box 163, Cambridge CB3 9PU U.K.

www.eerdmans.com/youngreaders

Manufactured at Worzalla, Stevens Point, Wisconsin, USA,
in July 2014; first printing

14 15 16 17 18 19 20 21   9 8 7 6 5 4 3 2 1

Library of Congress Cataloging-in-Publication Data

Dumon Tak, Bibi.
[Mikis de ezeljongen. English]
Mikis and the donkey / by Bibi Dumon Tak;
illustrated by Philip Hopman;
translated by Laura Watkinson.
pages cm
Originally published in Amsterdam by Querido in 2011 under the title,
Mikis de ezeljongen.
Summary: "Mikis is thrilled when his grandfather
buys a new donkey, but soon begins to worry that
he is overworking the animal" — Provided by publisher.
ISBN 978-0-8028-5430-8
[1. Donkeys — Fiction. 2. Grandfathers — Fiction.
3. Family life — Greece — Fiction. 4. Corfu Island (Greece) — Fiction.]
I. Hopman, Philip, illustrator. II. Watkinson, Laura. III. Title.
PZ7.D893635Mik 2014
[Fic] — dc23
2013044666

Nederlands
letterenfonds
dutch foundation
for literature

The publisher gratefully acknowledges the support
of the Dutch Foundation for Literature.

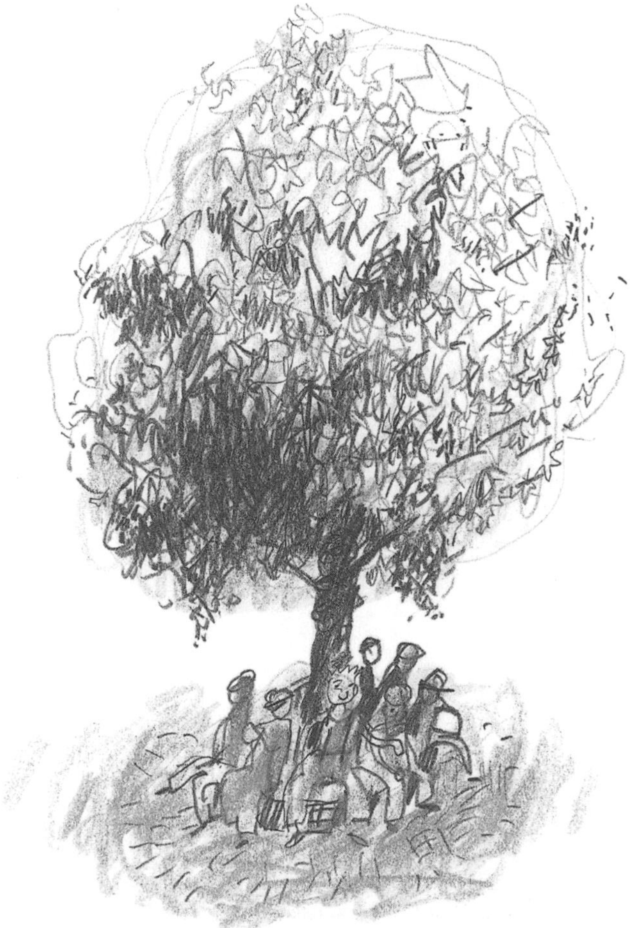

1

Grandpa was sitting under the big sycamore tree. It was impossible to miss him. He was always the one who did most of the talking. And whenever he talked, he waved his arms around in the air like he was trying to shoo away a bunch of flies.

"Pappou!" cried Mikis when he saw his grandpa.

"Shouldn't you be at school?" asked Grandpa.

"School is done for today, Pappou."

"Already?" said Grandpa. "You youngsters seem to spend more time playing than learning. When I was your age, we had to work out in the olive groves for hours, and take care of the animals too."

Grandpa threw his hands in the air again. His hair was as white as snow, but his eyebrows were as black as coal. Mikis sometimes used to give them a rub, because he was sure Grandpa dyed them, the way Grandma dyed her hair whenever she was going somewhere special.

"I have a surprise waiting for you at home," said Grandpa.

"What? What?" said Mikis, and he started running, even though he didn't know what the surprise was yet.

"Go see Yaya. I'll be there soon."

2

Mikis flew out of the village square. He raced up the narrow alleyways, left, right, up and up, past the house with a thousand flowers, around the corner, past the giant cactus, up the steps, through the doorway, and into the house, where he found Grandma busy with the big spring cleaning.

"Yaya," cried Mikis. He could hardly catch his breath. "Where's my surprise?"

Grandma told Mikis to sit quietly for a moment. She put a glass of cold water on the table in front of him.

"Drink this," she said. "You got here early."

"I ran all the way."

Grandma cut a slice of bread and spread it with jam. With his mouth still full, Mikis asked where the surprise was. He fidgeted on the chair. He crumpled up the tablecloth. Then his bread almost went down the wrong way and he coughed so much that he sent crumbs flying everywhere.

"Yaya, what is it?"

Grandma shook her head and looked at Mikis. "First finish your bread and jam, Mikis. And when you've calmed down you can go look . . . in the stable."

Mikis jumped to his feet, flew down the steps, and shot across the yard to the stable. But it was so dark in there that he couldn't see a thing.

"Hello?" said Mikis. He stood very still and listened.

But that didn't work, because all he could hear was himself panting. He took a few steps forward and bumped into the wooden planks of the pen where Grandpa kept the goats in the winter. He leaned against the wood and swallowed down the last pieces of bread.

Then he heard a rustling sound. Mikis stood on tiptoes and tried to look over the top of the planks. All he could see was black, but within that darkness was one spot that was even darker. He saw two long ears sticking up above the planks. Mikis found a stool and climbed up onto it.

"Well?" Mikis heard a voice behind him. Grandpa and Grandma were standing in the doorway with their arms around each other's shoulders.

"Is it for me?" asked Mikis.

Grandpa and Grandma started laughing.

"What next?" they said. "That donkey has to work. It's not a pet or a playmate, Mikis!"

Mikis stroked the donkey's ears. It was six feet from the bottom of the ears to their very tip . . . and then six feet all the way back down again. Well, that's what it felt like. The donkey's ears were so long that there seemed to be no end to them!

"Come here," said Grandpa. "You can sit on her back for a little while." Grandpa lifted Mikis over the planks and put him down on the donkey's warm back.

"You'll need to think of a name for her," he said. "And don't forget she's a girl."

3

Mikis ran his hands through the donkey's soft fur. Grandpa and Grandma had gone back inside for something to eat. "How come you don't have a name yet?" asked Mikis.

But the donkey didn't reply. She just shuffled around the stable. Mikis slid down from her back. He tickled her neck, stroked her mane, and said, "Weren't you important enough to have a name?"

The donkey licked the planks. Mikis could see her more clearly now. She was brown and her nose was paler, almost white. "Of course you're important," said Mikis. "In fact, you're so important that we have to come up with a very fine name for you. And you're going to help me." Mikis held the donkey's halter and took a good look at her. "I'm going to list five hundred names now. If you hear a name you like, you have to blink."

Mikis thought about all the famous singers he'd ever heard of. And he thought about the girls at school, and their moms, and their grandmas. And he tried to remember all the prettiest names from the stories that his teacher, Miss Chrysi, had told the class.

"Okay," he said to the donkey. "This is important. This is for the rest of your life. Do you understand?"

The donkey just stared at Mikis.

"Then let's begin," he said. "You have to concentrate

Tsaki   Zenovia   Fotini

Pandora   Varvara   Sotiria

Thessaloniki   Amarante   Rita

Delfi   Miffy   Zefiros

really hard. I'm going to start with a test name, just to prac-
tice. To see if you understand. So this isn't a real name yet.
When you hear a name you like, you're going to blink. But
no blinking until then. Okay?"

Mikis came up with a test name, a name he'd never heard
before. He put his mouth up close to the donkey's ear and he
whispered, "Tsaki."

The donkey was startled. She took a step back . . . and she
blinked.

"Good. So you understand what you need to do," said
Mikis. He knew donkeys weren't stupid. Then he started listing a whole lot of names.

"Zenovia, Fotini, Pandora, um . . . Varvara. You have to
blink, remember? Filadelfia, Julia, um . . ."

The donkey stood still and listened to Mikis. But

she didn't react at all. She just looked at Mikis with big, unblinking eyes as he said the names more and more loudly.

"Sotiria, Amarante, Thessaloniki, Rita, Miffy, Delfi."

Mikis suggested a whole load of weird and wonderful names, but the donkey didn't even twitch. Her ears pointed straight up, like towers.

"Zefiros," shouted Mikis. But that didn't count, because it was a boy's name.

"Elena." He hoped the donkey wouldn't blink this time, because Elena was a girl in his class. She was the nicest girl in his class, and he didn't want to have to tell her that he'd named Grandma and Grandpa's donkey after her.

Finally Mikis ran out of names.

So he said "Tsaki" again. And the donkey blinked.

4

"Aren't you done yet?" asked Grandpa, coming into the stable.

Mikis told him it had taken a long time, but he and the donkey had finally agreed.

"Agreed? What do you mean?" asked Grandpa. "That donkey helped you to decide?"

"Of course," said Mikis.

"Since when do donkeys get a say in what they're called?"

Mikis shrugged his shoulders. Grandpa took Mikis's hand and led him out of the stable and to the kitchen, where Grandma gave him a piece of baklava to eat.

"So?" she asked. "What did you decide?"

"He let the donkey choose for itself," said Grandpa.

Grandma frowned at Grandpa. "What do you mean?" she asked.

Grandpa told her that Mikis and the donkey had come up with a name together.

"Together?" asked Grandma.

"I think the donkey was allowed to vote," said Grandpa.

"To vote on the best name?"

Grandpa nodded.

"Do you actually want to know what her name is?" said Mikis.

"Of course. Out with it, my boy," said Grandpa.

"The donkey's name is . . . Tsaki."

Grandma and Grandpa started to laugh. They'd never heard such a strange name before, but Grandpa smiled and said, "That's a fine name, Mikis. Now run along home, or Mom and Dad will be worried."

"See you tomorrow," said Mikis.

"Good, good. And when you come tomorrow, you can go for a little ride on Tsaki."

5

Mikis lay awake in bed for a long time that night, staring up at the ceiling. His room was pitch dark, so there wasn't much to look at. But Mikis could still see all kinds of things. He could see himself sitting on a donkey. A donkey that didn't want to be called Varvara, or Filadelfia, or Amarante. A donkey that had chosen a little name for herself, nothing fancy. Mikis knew for sure that the donkey in Grandpa's stable understood him perfectly well. And he knew that she had thought, *I'm just a working donkey. I don't need a fancy name. Tsaki's good enough for me.*

Mikis lay awake for so long thinking about Tsaki that his mom had to shake him awake the next morning.

"Hey, Mikis, what's up?" she said. "It's like you're on another planet." But Mikis rubbed his eyes and told his mom that he was at home, as usual, in the village of Liapades, on the Greek island of Corfu, on planet Earth.

"Well, that's good," said Mom, and she gave him a hug.

"Do you think donkeys can talk, Mom?" he asked.

"What do you think?" his mom replied.

"Well, I think they can. But what about you?"

"If you think they can, then it's true," she said. "Now get dressed quickly or you'll be late for school."

Every day, all of the children in the class sat around in a circle for their morning meeting. Anyone who had done something special or interesting could tell the rest of the class about it. Miss Chrysi pointed at Elena, who was waving her hand in the air and seemed very eager to tell the rest of the class her news. Everyone could see she was wearing new shoes. They were bright pink.

"I have a new pair of shoes," she said. She spun around on the tips of her toes like a ballerina. All of the other children clapped.

Then it was Andreas's turn. He held up a tooth. "At last!" said Miss Chrysi. All of the children had a few gaps in their teeth, except for Andreas. He held up his tooth as proudly as if it was the World Cup. Everyone cheered.

"Does anyone else have interesting news?" asked Miss Chrysi.

"I do," said Mikis.

"What is it?" she asked. And Mikis told them about his grandpa's new donkey and said he'd been allowed to choose the name and that the donkey had helped.

"The donkey helped to choose its own name?" asked Miss Chrysi.

Mikis sighed.

"What's his name?" asked Nikos.

"Tsaki," said Mikis. "And she's a girl."

"Ah, a jenny. That's what female donkeys are called," said Miss Chrysi. She liked to teach the class new things whenever she could.

All the rest of the day, Mikis thought about Tsaki. New shoes were great. Losing a tooth was fun too. But a new donkey? That was the best thing in the whole wide world!

Grandpa was sitting under the sycamore tree again, with his hands dancing around his head. He was talking to his brother Vasilis. Uncle Vasilis was even older than Grandpa and he was stone deaf. He had hair growing out of his ears and sometimes he spat on the ground. He always said to Mikis, "My ears may be dead, but the rest of me is still going strong." And then he would laugh and laugh and laugh.

Mikis had no time for Uncle Vasilis's jokes right now. He asked Grandpa if he could go ride Tsaki.

Grandpa picked up Mikis and put him on his lap. Mikis was still just about small enough for that.

"Oof! You're growing so big now!" said Grandpa. Then he turned to his brother and yelled in his ear, "This is the boy who talks to donkeys."

"What?" said Uncle Vasilis. "The boy who talks to monkeys? Well, that makes sense. I've always said he was a cheeky little monkey!"

"Not monkeys! Donkeys!" shouted Grandpa. He put his hands to his head and pretended they were donkey ears, but Tsaki's ears were six times longer than Grandpa's hands and about ten times more beautiful.

Uncle Vasilis said, "Donkeys?" Grandpa nodded.

Mikis folded his arms and shouted, "Come on, Pappou!"

Grandpa stood up, slapped his brother on the shoulder,

and shuffled off across the village square, along the alleyways, up and up, past the house with a thousand flowers, around the corner, past the giant cactus, up the steps, through the doorway, and into the kitchen, where Grandma was peeling potatoes. And as they walked, Grandpa kept chuckling to himself and saying, "Yes, that's right. The boy who talks to donkeys."

Mikis said nothing. He held on to Grandpa's hand and thought to himself: *There's no point talking to Grandpa. He's too old for a good conversation.*

"Where are we going?" Mikis asked Grandpa. He was sitting on Tsaki's back and rocking gently from side to side.

"We're going up the mountain to fetch wood for the fire," said Grandpa.

"So we're not just going for a walk?"

"Walking is for folks who have nothing better to do."

Tsaki calmly plodded after Grandpa. Two baskets hung from her back, one on the left and one on the right. A rope was tied to her halter. She looked carefully to see where she was stepping on the steep, narrow path. Mikis stroked her bristly mane.

Grandpa owned a large piece of land up the mountain, where olive trees grew. He cut down the old trees and chopped them into logs. Now that it was spring, he wanted to stock up on firewood for the next winter. That would mean climbing up and down the mountain about fifty times.

"If we pile the wood up high in Tsaki's baskets," said Grandpa, "we'll only have to go up and down the mountain about forty times."

"Forty times?" Mikis was so surprised that he almost fell off Tsaki's back. "Pappou, do you know how many times that is?"

"Yes," said Grandpa. "It's a whole lot of times, but the higher we pile up the wood, the sooner we'll be done."

When they reached the olive grove, Grandpa tied Tsaki to a tree.

"If you pass me the logs," said Grandpa, "I'll stack them in the baskets."

After just a few minutes, Mikis was already boiling hot. Grandpa said it was going well. He kept on piling and piling up the wood and, after a while, Mikis told him that they had enough. But Grandpa said there was still room for more wood. Otherwise, they'd have to go up and down that mountain sixty times or more.

By the time Grandpa stopped, the donkey's baskets were bulging. Then he added a few branches to the top, because they were handy for starting the fire. You could hardly see Tsaki under all that wood. She looked like a tree on legs. Putting one hoof in front of the other, she set off down the mountain path.

Grandpa asked Mikis if he wanted to sit up among the branches on Tsaki's back, but Mikis thought Tsaki already had enough to carry. He held on tightly to her rope and said, "Come on, girl."

Grandpa, Mikis, and Tsaki worked until it was time to eat. They went up and down the mountain three times. When Tsaki was back in the stable, Mikis brought her a bucket of water before he drank any of his lemonade.

"You're a funny boy," said Grandma. "The donkey can wait." But Mikis said that Tsaki had carried at least her own weight in firewood down the mountain.

"Did you hear that?" said Grandma to Grandpa. "Before long, you're going to have to start paying that donkey wages."

"Yes," said Grandpa. "And then I'll have to open a bank account for her."

"And the donkey will have to learn how to sign checks."

Grandma and Grandpa laughed and slapped their knees. Mikis put his lemonade glass on the table and said, "I'll see you tomorrow." He had decided that it was better just to ignore old people who laughed at donkeys.

8

Every day after school Mikis went to Grandpa's to help him with the firewood. Three times up the mountain and three times back down again. On the tenth day, Grandpa said he had to take Grandma on the scooter to the optician's in the city. "Tsaki's ready to go. And you know the way," he said.

Mikis stared at Grandpa with his mouth wide open.

"What are you looking at me like that for?" Grandpa asked. "You can go fetch a few logs by yourself, can't you?" Mikis swallowed and was about to say something, but Grandpa beat him to it, "There's only one path up there, my boy, so you can't get lost. And when you've had enough, you can just park the donkey in the stable."

Mikis was so happy that he was almost glowing.

Grandpa said he didn't have to load the baskets full. Half-full was good enough. And if there were any problems, he was to go tell Uncle Vasilis.

When Grandma and Grandpa had gone, Mikis ran to the stable. Tsaki was ready and waiting, with the baskets on her back.

"Tsaki," Mikis whispered in her ear. He tickled her neck, tied the rope to her halter, and led her out of the stable. Tsaki blinked in the bright light.

"Come along," said Mikis. Tsaki pushed her nose into Mikis's back and they slowly made their way up the mountain path.

Mikis thought ten logs in each basket was more than enough. "You've already worked so hard this week," he said to Tsaki.

Halfway back down, Mikis stopped for a moment to swat away some flies and to ask if Tsaki was doing all right. Tsaki didn't reply. "Would you like to go on walking?" asked Mikis. He took a few steps downhill, and Tsaki walked along with him. Mikis stopped again and said, "Do you know what? I'm going to untie you."

Mikis removed the rope from Tsaki's halter and started walking again. Tsaki followed him — all the way back to the yard. Mikis didn't tie her up again. She stood there, perfectly still, waiting as Mikis emptied the baskets. Then he gave her a piece of bread and whispered in her one of her long ears, "You know something, Tsaki? You're my best friend."

When Grandma and Grandpa got home, Mikis could see how proud they were of him. "Mikis the donkey boy," said Grandpa as he got off his scooter.

"So? Did the two of you have a nice chat while we were gone?" asked Grandma.

Mikis told them that Tsaki didn't need the rope any longer. "She's like a magnet," he said. "She follows me wherever I go." Grandpa gave Mikis a big glass of lemonade.

"Are you going to be here all day tomorrow?" asked Grandpa. Mikis nodded. Of course he'd be there all day. And the day after that, and the next day, until there were no days left. But that was a few centuries away. By that time, Mikis would be a grown-up himself and have his own stable full of donkeys, with names that they'd helped to choose.

Mikis's mom and dad always slept late on Saturdays. Their store was open only on weekdays. They sold cigarettes, detergent, cheese, handkerchiefs, water, matches, and candy — more or less everything a person could need.

Mikis sneaked out of the house while it was still dark and made his way to Grandma and Grandpa's house. They gave him some breakfast and then he went to work with Grandpa.

Grandpa, Mikis, and Tsaki went up and down the mountain four times before lunch. Mikis kept asking over and over again, so Grandpa finally let Tsaki off the rope. Mikis walked ahead, followed by Tsaki, with Grandpa bringing up the rear. When Tsaki didn't walk fast enough, Grandpa slapped her on the hindquarters.

Tsaki shuffled down the mountain. She kept on walking slowly and carefully, whether Grandpa slapped her or not. Mikis told Grandpa that he'd overloaded the baskets. But Grandpa said they'd be working for a month otherwise, as they had so much firewood to move. "You don't let a truck go out half empty, do you, boy?"

"But Tsaki's not a truck, is she?"

"Ha, young man," said Grandpa. "That's where you're wrong."

Mikis stopped walking. Tsaki bumped into him, and Mikis nearly went tumbling down the mountain.

"But, Pappou," said Mikis, turning around. He tried to look at his grandpa, but Tsaki and her massive load of firewood were in the way.

"Just you keep walking, young man!" shouted Grandpa. He gave Tsaki a tap and they were off again.

As they were unloading the baskets, Grandpa told Mikis that he would have bought a tractor if he were richer. "But now I have a donkey instead," he said. "A tractor on legs. Do you understand?"

"But, Pappou . . ."

"No buts, my boy. Donkeys fit on narrow mountain paths, they don't guzzle gas, and they usually start the first time."

At the end of the day, the three of them were worn out from all that hard work.

"Tomorrow's Sunday," said Grandpa, "so we're not working."

"Oh, that's too bad," said Mikis, who was going to miss his friend.

"But I have an idea," said Grandpa. "Tomorrow, Tsaki's all yours."

Mikis could hardly sleep that night. He was thinking about all the things he could do with Tsaki, and he couldn't decide what would be most fun. It took him a while, but finally he decided: he and Tsaki were going to go on a world tour!

"Do you know what time it is?" asked Mom as Mikis filled his backpack very early the next morning.

"Is it that donkey again?" Dad shouted from the bedroom. Mikis ran out of the house before his parents could stop him. The sun hadn't even come up yet. The air was fresh and it tingled in his nose. He could feel that spring was just beginning.

Grandma and Grandpa lived on the other side of the village, but the village was so small that it took almost no time to run from one side to the other. Breathe in and out ten times and you were there.

When Mikis got to Grandma and Grandpa's house, the water for the tea was already boiling.

"Ah, donkey boy," said Grandpa. "You're bright and early."

"I'm going on a world tour!" said Mikis.

"And where is this world tour going to take you?"

"We're starting at the olive grove. And after that, we'll see."

"We?" asked Grandma.

"Tsaki and I."

"Oh yes, of course," said Grandma. "The two of you decide everything together, don't you?" She looked at Grandpa and gave him a wink. Mikis pretended not to notice.

Grandpa said he'd put Tsaki's baskets on for Mikis. "She can carry your lunch for you."

Mikis told him it was Tsaki's day off and that he could carry his things on his own back.

Before he set off, Grandma put a bottle of water, a box of juice, and a sandwich into his backpack. Then she looked anxiously at Grandpa.

"To the olive grove and back," said Grandpa. "And that's it. Make it a small world tour."

They walked to the stable together. Grandpa tied the rope to Tsaki's halter and waved the end of the rope in front of Mikis's nose. "You're not to untie her. Keep her on this rope. You understand?"

Mikis nodded and started walking up the mountain with Tsaki, on a small world tour.

The only sound on the path up to the olive grove was the clip-clop of Tsaki's hoofs. They walked very slowly, because it was Tsaki's day off.

Mikis asked Tsaki if she liked walking without the baskets on her back. He asked if she was too hot. He asked if she was thirsty.

Tsaki didn't answer, but just plodded along behind him like she was sleepwalking. She didn't seem to be enjoying herself. It was almost as if she preferred to lug around her weight in firewood, even on her day off.

Mikis had forgotten what Grandpa had said, and he untied the rope. "Is that better?" he asked. Tsaki just pushed her nose into Mikis's back, and they walked the rest of the way to the olive grove. Mikis knew there was a patch of grass up there. Delicious green grass.

As soon as they got there, Tsaki lowered her nose and took a big mouthful of grass. Mikis sat down against a tree and drank his juice. Then he had all of his water and ate his sandwich. The sun was nice and warm, but Mikis didn't even think about stopping for a little nap. There was no time to waste.

"Come on, Tsaki," he said after a while. "We're on a world tour. And we still have a long way to go." He stroked her neck, rubbed her sides, but then suddenly . . . *Thwack!*

Tsaki kicked out at him with one of her back legs, as if she wanted to push him away.

Startled, Mikis jumped back and saw blood on his hand. But Tsaki hadn't touched him. It wasn't his blood. So where had it come from? Carefully, Mikis kneeled down and looked under Tsaki's belly. He could see a big cut beside her front leg — and the cut was bleeding.

It's all Grandpa's fault, thought Mikis. Grandpa had loaded a million tons of firewood on Tsaki's back without thinking about whether she could carry that much. Mikis looked on the other side of Tsaki's belly. There was blood there too.

"Poor Tsaki," said Mikis. And he kept on saying the same thing, in a calming voice, all the way down the mountain. He wasn't in the mood for a world tour anymore.

Tsaki trudged along behind Mikis like a little old lady. When they got back to the yard, Mikis didn't know what to do. He couldn't ask Grandma and Grandpa for help. They would just laugh and say that tractors sometimes got a bit rusty as well.

Mikis tied the rope to Tsaki's halter again and pulled her along, down the path into the village. But Tsaki wasn't at all happy about walking past her stable and she stood there, stubbornly refusing to move.

"You're too good for Grandpa," said Mikis. "He doesn't look after you like he should. Don't you realize that?" Tsaki stayed where she was. Why should she walk down a path she didn't know? She just wanted to go home.

For a moment, Mikis thought about slapping her, so that she'd start walking. But then he'd be acting just like Grandpa, and he didn't want that. He pulled on the rope as hard as he could. But Tsaki still wouldn't budge.

Then Tsaki slowly started to step backward in the direction of her stable.

"Come on!" cried Mikis. But the harder he pulled, the more Tsaki wanted to go into the yard.

Mikis saw someone coming in the distance. He could tell it was Elena. Anyone could have seen her pink shoes all the way from the moon.

"Where are you going?" she asked.

"To the doctor's," said Mikis.

Elena asked if he was sick, but he pointed at the blood on Tsaki's tummy. Elena's face went completely white. Mikis thought she was about to faint.

"Could you hold onto Tsaki for a moment?" He handed Elena the rope and went to pick some grass. And then he slowly tempted Tsaki to move forward. Step by step, until she could no longer see her stable.

Elena went with Mikis. They walked along the alleyways and followed the path down the hill. There was no one around. Even the village square was empty.

"It's Sunday," said Elena.

"So?" said Mikis.

"It's the doctor's day off."

"Not if someone's bleeding to death."

Elena nodded.

Mikis tied Tsaki to the fence in front of the doctor's house and knocked on the door, quietly because it was the doctor's day off.

"You'll have to knock louder," said Elena.

So Mikis started banging the door and shouting at the top of his voice: "Doctor! Doctor!" Then, finally, they heard footsteps in the hallway, and the front door swung open.

"Mikis!" the doctor exclaimed. "There's nothing wrong with Grandma or Grandpa, is there?"

Mikis shook his head and pointed at the donkey. The doctor looked at Tsaki and raised his eyebrows.

"She's hurt," said Mikis.

"Who is?" replied the doctor.

"Tsaki."

"You mean the donkey?"

Mikis nodded.

"But you know I'm not a veterinarian, don't you?"

"The vet lives four villages away," said Mikis. "And Tsaki needs help now."

The doctor asked where Grandpa was. He sounded very stern. Mikis almost started crying. He told the doctor that it was Grandpa who had broken the donkey.

"Broken the donkey?" said the doctor. His expression already seemed kinder. "This is an animal, not a car."

Mikis told him that Grandpa called his donkey a tractor on legs.

The doctor shook his head. "Let's take a look, then," he said. He walked over to Tsaki and he saw what the problem was right away. "I think Grandpa's been overloading his tractor."

The doctor hurried inside and came back with some absorbent cotton and a jar of ointment. He treated Tsaki's cuts. When he was done, he placed his hands on Mikis's shoulders, looked at him, and said, "You're a good boy, Mikis." Then he stroked Tsaki and told Mikis how to take good care of the donkey's wounds. "Rub this in twice a day. Put a blanket under the baskets and don't load them too full from now on. And be sure to tell your grandpa."

Mikis shook the doctor's hand.

"Oh, yes," said the doctor, "and you can also tell him that the donkey needs a whole week of vacation."

As Mikis walked across the village square with Elena and Tsaki, he felt really light, as if he'd put down a load of a hundred tons of wood.

Then he heard someone yelling from beneath the sycamore. "Hey, squirt!" It echoed across the square, from the church to the houses opposite. Mikis froze. The square was full of people now and every single one of them was looking at him. Where had they all suddenly come from? Then he realized that the church service had just finished.

Grandpa came storming toward them. Mikis didn't know his grandpa could still move that fast. When Grandpa reached them, his face was red and sweaty. And he had hardly any breath left in his lungs. Grandpa reached out and grabbed Mikis's ear.

"Where have you been?" Grandpa growled.

Mikis couldn't say anything.

"I said up the path to the olive grove! And no farther!"

"But, Pappou . . ."

"Does this look like a mountain path?"

Mikis's bottom lip started to tremble.

"So what are you doing here with that donkey?" Spit was flying out of Grandpa's mouth, right into Mikis's face. As he spoke, Grandpa held on tightly to Mikis's ear, and so Mikis had to take a step forward. Tsaki immediately did the same.

She followed Mikis, because that's what she always did. Because she was a magnet, as Mikis had said.

Everyone on the square had stopped talking. All of the churchgoers were looking at Grandpa, who was pulling Mikis by the ear, and at the donkey, who was still following him, even though Mikis had dropped the rope.

No one knew whether it was because of Tsaki or because of Elena bursting into tears or because of Mikis taking out the jar of ointment that the doctor had given him, but Grandpa calmed down.

"What do you have there?" he asked. He took the jar of ointment from Mikis and tried to read the label. The word was about a hundred letters long and looked impossible to pronounce.

"The doctor gave it to me," said Mikis.

Then Uncle Vasilis started interfering and told his brother to think about his heart. "We were worried about you, young man." Uncle Vasilis had to shout so that he could hear himself. "We went to look for you, but you'd vanished. Poof! Donkey and all."

"I went to see Doctor Papadakis," said Mikis.

"Papadakis?" said Grandpa. "So who's sick?"

"Tsaki." Mikis pointed at the cuts on Tsaki's tummy. "It's because of the baskets."

For a moment, Grandpa was speechless. More and more people were coming to see what was going on. Uncle Vasilis shouted loud enough for everyone to hear, "Did you really take that donkey to see a human doctor?" He laughed so hard that his false teeth almost went clattering onto the cobbles.

Elena had stopped sobbing. Mikis looked at Grandpa and held his breath. Grandpa gazed around at his brother

and at all the other people who were standing around in the square. He had let go of Mikis's ear. Then he shook his head and said, "Well, if that doesn't take the cake."

14

Mikis had to give donkey lessons to his grandpa.

"Pappou, those baskets make her sore and the strap is far too tight."

"So what should I do, my boy?"

"You need to put a blanket under them. And you shouldn't load the baskets so full. Tsaki's not a truck."

"Who said she was?"

"You did. And you said Tsaki's a tractor on legs. But that's not true. Oh, and she's not allowed to work all this week."

"Where did you get that idea?"

"Doctor's orders."

"Well I'll be . . ." said Grandpa. "Did the doctor really say that?"

Mikis nodded.

"Ha, that's easy for him to say. He drives around in a nice Ford."

"You have to rub it in twice a day," Mikis continued, and he put the jar of ointment on Grandma and Grandpa's kitchen table.

The news that Mikis had taken Tsaki to see Doctor Papadakis on a Sunday soon spread all over the village. When he was sitting in the morning meeting at school on Monday, he didn't even have to tell the story himself. Andreas told everyone, because he'd heard it from his dad. Elena filled in the details.

Their teacher lived in the city and she hadn't heard the news yet. She didn't know what to make of it at all. "What?" she said. "Mikis took Tsaki to the human doctor? On Sunday?"

The whole class started nodding.

"On Sunday?"

Mikis didn't understand why everyone had to keep mentioning that. "Tsaki almost bled to death. I had no choice," he said.

During their art class, Miss Chrysi told everyone to draw Tsaki. The children all thought that was a great idea. Andreas drew a donkey with so much blood that it looked like Tsaki had been hit by a cannonball. Aliki drew the doctor giving Tsaki an injection. Nikos made a picture of a donkey lying in a pool of blood. Anna drew a donkey in an ambulance with a flashing light. Nitsa's donkey was lying on its back with all four legs sticking up in the air. Elena drew Tsaki with Mikis standing beside her, wearing a big medal around his neck. And Mikis drew Tsaki grazing beneath an olive tree with the sun setting behind her.

15

After that Sunday, everyone — not just Grandma and Grandpa — started to call Mikis the donkey boy. And it wasn't because he was stupid, or slow, or stubborn. It was because he had rescued a donkey.

Every day after school Mikis went to visit Tsaki. Sometimes Elena went with him. She said it was because donkeys were her favorite animal, but secretly it was because Mikis was her favorite boy in the class. But of course she never said so. She knew better than that.

On Sundays, Mikis was allowed to go out for a walk with Tsaki — not only up the mountain path, but around the whole village. Before they went out, he brushed Tsaki and cleaned her hoofs. He checked to see that Grandpa had been using the blanket and that he hadn't been overfilling the baskets that week.

Spring was already well under way when Mikis said to Grandpa one Saturday morning, "Can Tsaki have a window?"

Grandpa looked at Mikis for a long time and said, "What is there for that animal to look at?"

"Nothing," said Mikis. "It's just that it's so dark in the stable."

Grandpa rubbed his face. Mikis knew that meant he was thinking. To help him out, Mikis said they could just knock a hole in the wall and put a window in it.

Grandpa nodded. "A window for the donkey," he muttered.

"You don't have to do it right now," said Mikis.

"No, no," said Grandpa.

"What she really needs is a whole new stable," said Mikis. "One that's not so drafty in the winter."

"So a new window isn't enough?"

"Not really."

"Before we know it, our donkey will be living in a palace," said Grandpa, "and we'll be living in a shack."

Mikis knew there was no chance of a new stable for Tsaki. Even just a window seemed to be asking for too much. So Mikis came up with another plan for making Tsaki's life more interesting. And he was going to need Elena's help. He went over to Elena's to tell her about his idea.

16

The next morning Mikis and Tsaki were waiting beneath the sycamore tree. They had been standing there for a quarter of an hour by the time Elena got there. It wasn't because she was late. Mikis had arrived way too early, because he was so excited.

If Grandpa didn't even want to put a window in the dark, musty stable, then Tsaki might as well forget about a completely new stable. They would have to find a different way to cheer up Tsaki. They were going to go out and find her a friend, and Mikis knew just the place to look.

In a field beside the road to the beach lived a donkey belonging to Kostas, who had a restaurant down by the sea. He used to get the donkey to move things across the sand for him. But now he had a big Jeep and he didn't need the donkey anymore. *If we go visit Kostas's lonely donkey, we'll make two donkeys happy,* Mikis thought.

Tsaki walked along behind Mikis and Elena. They didn't need the rope, because Tsaki followed Mikis wherever he went. Her hoofs tapped happily along the road. She took a good look around. She could do that now that she didn't have to carry any heavy baskets and now that no one was telling her to keep on walking.

Halfway there, Tsaki suddenly stopped in the middle of the road. She sniffed the air and then she started to bray. She

brayed so loudly that Mikis and Elena had to cover their ears. When she stopped, she stood there, with her head raised and her ears high.

And then, there was a reply in the distance. It was Kostas's donkey. There was no holding Tsaki. She just took off! Down the road, around the corner, and out of sight.

Mikis and Elena ran after her, but they couldn't run nearly as fast as Tsaki. There must have been a rocket hidden beneath that grey coat. She could travel faster than the speed of sound! By the time they got to Kostas's olive grove, Mikis and Elena were exhausted. They saw that part of the wooden fence had been knocked down, and Kostas's donkey's rope was dangling from the tree. But the two donkeys were nowhere in sight!

17

"What now?" asked Elena.

"We go look for them," said Mikis. And they headed into the olive grove, where they found a shed. They walked all the way around the shed and looked inside. There were no donkeys to be seen. Mikis shouted Tsaki's name, but that didn't help. Donkeys aren't like dogs and they don't come running when you call them.

The olive grove was huge. There must have been a thousand trees! Mikis and Elena headed up the hill. They didn't say anything else to each other, because they were concentrating on the climb and thinking about Tsaki. Mikis didn't dare to think about Grandpa. It wasn't that long ago that Grandpa had almost pulled off Mikis's left ear. This time Grandpa was going to take hold of both his ears and never let him go. But that wasn't the worst of it. Losing Tsaki was far, far worse.

The hill never seemed to end. Elena's hair hung in tangles around her face, and the dust had turned her pink shoes dull.

"You go that way," said Mikis, "and I'll go this way."

Elena nodded. She didn't say anything. Mikis could see drops of water on her cheeks. *It's the heat,* he thought. But then he realized she was crying.

Kostas's olive grove seemed to be bigger than the whole island of Corfu! There was no end to it. And all the trees looked the same. The stupid things stood around like they were waiting for something. But what could they be waiting for? For the few olives that grew on their branches every year? Mikis didn't like olives. He liked moussaka and he liked baklava. But he couldn't stand olives. "It's a grown-up flavor," Grandma always said. "You'll like them when you're an adult." But Mikis didn't believe a word of it. Once awful, always awful. Then he heard someone calling his name. Mikis turned around and saw Elena waving in the distance. And she wasn't just waving. She was dancing too.

18

"We won't tell Grandma and Grandpa," said Mikis when he reached Elena. "And we won't tell anyone at school either. We'll never talk about this again. Promise?"

Elena nodded.

"Shake on it," said Mikis.

So Mikis and Elena shook hands. This was a promise that they meant to keep.

Then Mikis looked at Tsaki, who was standing cozily beside Kostas's donkey, as if nothing had happened.

"She must have been really lonely," said Mikis. "That's why she ran off like that." He tied the rope to her halter again and gave the other end to Elena.

"They were getting along really well back there," said Elena. "Really, really well."

Mikis took hold of Kostas's donkey and they started the walk back. Tsaki had to go first, or Kostas's donkey refused to move. When they got back, Mikis tied Kostas's donkey to the tree and said he'd come visit him again, but without Tsaki. Then Mikis and Elena put the fence back up and headed home.

Grandpa and Uncle Vasilis were sitting under the sycamore tree.

"Aha!" cried Uncle Vasilis. "Here come Joseph and Mary and the donkey."

Mikis sighed and Elena said that Christmas was ages ago. They walked quickly across the square to take Tsaki back to her stable as soon as possible. They climbed up along the narrow alleyways, left, right, up and up, past the house with a thousand flowers, around the corner, past the giant cactus, and into the yard, where Tsaki headed straight for her dark stable. Anyone could see she'd had enough excitement for one day.

The next morning at school, Mikis and Elena kept their mouths firmly shut when their teacher asked if anyone had done anything interesting. Andreas put his hand up.

"Tell us your story, then," said Miss Chrysi.

"Your hair looks funny, Miss."

Miss Chrysi reached up to touch her curls and asked if the other children thought her hair looked funny too. Everyone nodded, including Mikis and Elena. They were so relieved that no one could see they had a secret.

Miss Chrysi blushed. She asked what was so funny about her hair.

"It's flat," said Andreas.

"It doesn't usually look like that," said Spiros.

"Okay," said Miss Chrysi. She shook her head. "How about now?"

"Now it isn't quite so flat," said Andreas.

Miss Chrysi sighed and said, "It's because I was wearing a helmet this morning."

All of the children wanted to know if she'd bought a scooter.

She shook her head. "I came to school on the back of a motorbike this morning," she said. Miss Chrysi told them that she had a new boyfriend and that he had a motorbike. Everyone raced to the window, but Miss Chrysi told them that her boyfriend wasn't waiting in the schoolyard, and neither was his motorbike. "We'll have another chat tomorrow in our morning meeting and maybe, just maybe, I'll tell you some more about it then," said Miss Chrysi. "But now, we have work to do!"

Mikis picked up his math book. His teacher had found a friend and so had Tsaki. He couldn't take Tsaki's friend away now. That would be so mean. Mikis decided that he would go visit Kostas's donkey very soon — and not on his own, but with Tsaki.

And with Elena, if she felt brave enough.

19

"Are you sure we should be leaving those donkeys alone together?" asked Elena.

"But they got along well last time, didn't they?" said Mikis.

"Yes, they did," said Elena. "Really, really well."

"So it'll be fine," said Mikis.

"Okay, then," said Elena. "If you're sure."

That Sunday they kept a tight hold on Tsaki as they walked down the road where Kostas's donkey lived. They were both pretty nervous. Tsaki had pricked up her ears, but she didn't start braying this time. She just kept on walking and looking around as if she'd never been there before.

When they got to the olive grove, Kostas's donkey was standing there, staring into the distance, but then he spotted Tsaki and he brayed. *EE-AW! EE-AW!* Tsaki didn't reply and she didn't try to run to him. Just to make sure, Mikis and Elena held on to both sides of her halter.

Mikis opened the gate and tied up Tsaki beside Kostas's donkey. They sniffed at each other and then they both looked at Mikis and Elena. They seemed perfectly happy to stay where they were this time. Mikis and Elena were so relieved that they didn't notice someone coming closer. But then a deep, rumbling voice shouted at them and asked them what on earth they were up to. Mikis and Elena nearly jumped out of their skin. Even the donkeys seemed to be shaking.

It was Kostas. "Ah, it's the donkey boy," he boomed.

"We're just visiting," said Mikis.

Kostas folded his arms and took a good look. Then he said, "And, if I might ask, who exactly are you visiting?"

"Um, well," said Mikis, "you know, your donkey."

Kostas laughed and his tummy started to wobble. Mikis looked at Elena. Her face had gone completely white.

"So, are they enjoying their visit?" asked Kostas, nodding at the donkeys.

"Tsaki and your donkey were both lonely," said Mikis.

"And we thought . . ."

But Kostas didn't care about any of that. Nobody puts two tractors together in the barn to keep each other company, do they? Kostas was just the same as Grandpa! But luckily, he was also kind like Grandpa. He smiled and said, "I've got an idea. Why don't you take Peppi out for a walk too? Then you'll both have a donkey to lead."

"Peppi?" said Elena.

"Yes, that's my donkey's name," replied Kostas.

Mikis and Elena promised not to go out onto the road, but to stay in the olive grove. "When you've finished your walk, you must tie Peppi up. And make sure you don't get lost. My olive grove is huge," said Kostas. But Mikis and Elena already knew that from their last visit.

After that, Mikis and Elena went to visit Peppi every Sunday. Sometimes Andreas went with them, or Spiros. Mom came once, and so did Dad. And Grandma and Grandpa. The two donkeys had lots and lots of visitors, in fact. Even Miss Chrysi and her boyfriend came by on the motorbike one day. And everyone said, "When Mikis grows up, he's going to start a donkey farm."

And Mikis said, "Yes, I'm going to buy the whole island and fill it with donkeys."

"And what about us?" asked Grandpa.

"You can stay if you promise to behave yourselves," said Mikis.

20

It was the last day of school before the summer vacation. All of the children took a turn at talking about what they were going to do during vacation. Elena was staying at home, because her parents owned a hotel where lots of tourists came to stay, and they had to work extra hard in the summer months. Spiros was going to visit his big brother in Athens. Andreas was helping out his dad at the garage. Anna was going with her mom and dad to see her grandma in America. And Miss Chrysi said that she and her boyfriend were going to tour Italy on his motorbike.

"What about you, Mikis?" she asked.

"I'm going to build a new stable for Tsaki with Grandpa."

"With air-conditioning?" asked Andreas.

"Yes," said Mikis, "and with a conveyor belt."

"A conveyor belt?" asked Miss Chrysi.

"So Grandma can send fresh bread and apples directly from the kitchen to Tsaki's stable."

"So it's going to be a five-star stable," said Miss Chrysi.

It was boiling hot in the classroom, and all of the windows were open. Miss Chrysi kept on looking out of the window, as if she was expecting someone. She didn't even tell the children to take out their things or to get down to work. And her hair was looking quite flat again. Then she looked out of the window for what must have been the thousandth time and said, "Ah, there he is."

Everyone ran to the window. They heard a sputtering sound. *Chugchugchugchug.* It was Miss Chrysi's boyfriend on his motorbike. At last!

Miss Chrysi told all of the children to go outside because she had a surprise for them. They stood in a circle around Miss Chrysi's boyfriend. He said hi to the class and told them his name was Yorgos. Then he took a huge bag of popsicles out of his backpack and handed them around.

When the children had finished their popsicles, Miss Chrysi said to Andreas, "Would you like to cool down a bit?" She put her helmet on Andreas's head and he hopped up onto the motorbike behind Yorgos and they zoomed around the yard. Then everyone else was allowed to have a turn, one at a time. Yorgos was kept very busy for a while.

As Mikis and Elena were walking home for the last time before their summer vacation, Elena said, "Going on a motorbike is fun, but it's not as much fun as sitting on Tsaki's back."

Mikis looked at Elena and didn't say a word. He just thought: *When I grow up, I'm going to marry her.*

21

One evening, just before the start of the vacation, Grandpa had said, "Mikis, I have another surprise for you." And he had told him that he wanted to build a stable for Tsaki, but he couldn't do it on his own, so Mikis would have to help. Grandpa said, "If you want to have a donkey farm when you're older, we should really start building already."

Mikis was so happy that he rushed to tell Tsaki. The sun was still low in the sky, but Tsaki was already asleep. She shook her head when Mikis whispered in her ear that she was going to have a new home.

So, that very first day of the summer vacation, Mikis was standing on Grandma and Grandpa's doorstep, bright and early. Grandma poured Mikis a glass of milk. "You have until September," she said. "Why the hurry?"

"The sooner the stable's ready," said Mikis, "the sooner Tsaki will be able to enjoy it."

Grandpa agreed with Mikis, and so they set to work right after breakfast. They found the perfect spot for the new stable and they started measuring.

"The stable has to have its own yard," said Mikis.

"A yard?"

"So she can go outside whenever she wants to."

Grandpa sighed. "Does it need a balcony and a stoop too?"

"Hmm," said Mikis. "There's no need for a balcony, but she does want a guestroom."

"A guestroom? Who for?"

"For Peppi."

Grandpa shook his head. "Before you know it, Peppi will move in, and then there'll be another little donkey, and another, and another."

Mikis nodded and said, "That's the whole point of a donkey farm, Pappou!"

22

Grandpa had ordered all of the things they needed from the city. A truck pulled into the yard with a load of planks, sacks of cement, and zinc for the roof. There wasn't a conveyor belt, but there was wood for a new feeding trough and glass for the windows.

"We're not going to build a stoop, but we are going to make a yard for her with a little shelter," said Grandpa. Mikis thought that sounded like a good idea. "And the top half of the stable door will open so that Tsaki can look outside."

That summer, Mikis learned how to knock nails into planks, how to use a spirit level to make sure that everything was straight, how to mix cement for a strong floor, how to put in a window, how to put screws into wood, and how to saw a door in two.

Some days Andreas came over to help when he'd had enough of his dad's cars. On other days they stopped building because Grandpa and Tsaki had to go out to work. And sometimes Mikis went with Tsaki and Elena to visit Peppi. Mikis and Elena helped out in her parents' hotel too, cleaning tables and collecting empty glasses. And Mom and Dad came over to see Tsaki some evenings when they were done with their work at the store. Something different happened every day. It was the best vacation Mikis had ever had.

When the vacation was over and they had almost finished

building the stable, Mikis did a drawing of Tsaki's new house. He wrote the word *PARTY* under the picture. It was an invitation for the whole village to come see Tsaki's new stable. He nailed the invitation to the sycamore tree in the village square and then he went and asked Grandma and Grandpa if it was actually okay for him to have a party.

They said it was fine.

Phew!

Grandma and Mom baked cakes. Dad and Grandpa got wine and olives and beer and sausages to cook on the fire. Mikis and Elena brushed Tsaki until she gleamed as she had never gleamed before. And Uncle Vasilis came with his accordion. The party could start!

Everyone from the village was there, even Doctor Papadakis. They stood around in Grandma and Grandpa's yard the same way they usually stood around in the village square. They talked and laughed and drank and acted like Tsaki wasn't even there.

So Mikis decided to do something about that. He climbed onto a chair and said, "Ahem! Ladies and gentlemen and boys and girls!"

No one heard him. Grandpa stood beside Mikis and shouted that everyone should be quiet for a moment. They did as they were told. Uncle Vasilis was the only one who didn't hear. He just went on playing his accordion.

Everyone looked at Mikis. He announced that the big moment had arrived: Tsaki was going to move into her new home.

Elena led Tsaki out of her dark and stuffy old stable. She looked so beautiful with the new halter that Mom had

bought for her and the flowers that Elena had laced into her mane. All of the people of Liapades started clapping.

Tsaki looked around with wide, astonished eyes and her ears pointing straight up. It must have been the first time in the history of Corfu that people had ever applauded a donkey!

"Come on, Tsaki!" said Mikis.

But Tsaki wasn't interested. She didn't want to go inside her new stable at all. Elena rushed to help, followed by Dad and Grandpa. They pushed Tsaki's hindquarters, but Tsaki wouldn't budge. The way she was looking at her new stable, anyone would have thought it was a monster! Andreas tried to tempt her inside with a piece of cake, and Elena tried talking to Tsaki in her very kindest voice. But it didn't help.

"Do you want me to go get Peppi?" asked Kostas.

"How about I fetch a car and tow her in?" asked Andreas's dad. But Mikis said Tsaki had to choose to walk in by herself or not at all. All Tsaki wanted to do was to go back to her old stable. It was already starting to get dark. Why did she need a new house? Tsaki had no idea what all the fuss was about.

When the party was over, everyone wished Mikis good luck. And Kostas said, "Try again tomorrow."

That night, Tsaki slept in her old, familiar stable. And Mikis thought: *I'll put some fresh grass in her new feeding trough tomorrow and then she'll be sure to move.*

23

The first day of school after the summer vacation got off to a good start. When Mikis and the other children arrived, they found Miss Chrysi already waiting for them in the classroom. They all looked at each other and started whispering excitedly. Miss Chrysi told them to pick a place in the circle for their morning meeting. All of the children picked up their chairs and sat in the same place as the year before.

Miss Chrysi said, "So, class, you're stuck with me for another year." She looked around the circle with a smile on her face. Her hair was very flat indeed.

"What happened to the new teacher who was supposed to be coming?" asked Andreas.

"She moved to a different island."

"Which one?" asked Spiros.

"Crete, I think, or Kos, or no, Lesbos. Actually, I can't remember," said Miss Chrysi.

"Zakynthos," said Nitsa.

"Rhodes," said Elena.

"Santorini," said Anna.

All of the children started listing the names of Greek islands. There are over a thousand Greek islands, so after about five minutes Miss Chrysi said that enough was enough and that they probably weren't planning to write to the other teacher anyway. "Or do you want to send her a letter?"

she asked.

"Of course we do," said Andreas. "To tell her she can stay on her new island."

All of the children laughed, and so did Miss Chrysi. They were so happy to have another whole new school year together.

"So, Mikis," said Miss Chrysi when everyone was quiet again. "How are things going with your stable?"

"The stable's fine," said Mikis.

"And is it finished?" she asked.

"Well, yes," said Mikis.

"But Tsaki doesn't want to go inside," said Elena.

"Not even if we push her," said Andreas.

Miss Chrysi said the class would have to work together that week to come up with a solution, or Mikis would have worked all summer vacation for nothing.

"You'll have to blindfold Tsaki," said Stefanos.

"Not now. This week," said Miss Chrysi. "Right now we have to work."

"A blindfold would be mean," said Elena.

"Demolish her old stable," said Spiros.

"Not now," said Miss Chrysi again.

"Tie her to the new stable with a really long rope and make the rope a little bit shorter every day," said Alexandros.

"Stop feeding her," said Nikos.

"Children . . ." said Miss Chrysi.

"I've just got to be patient," said Mikis. "That's all I can do."

"Now, get to your places! And be quick about it! March! Left, right, left, right!" said Miss Chrysi. That helped. All of the children leaped to their feet, picked up their chairs and took them back to exactly the same desks as last year. It was as if the summer vacation hadn't happened at all.

24

No one could get Tsaki to move into her new stable. One time, when it was raining and the cold was blowing in from the ocean, Mikis placed some bread just inside the door. Tsaki rushed over, put one foot inside the new stable, reached out her neck to grab the bread, gobbled it down, and then dashed back out into the rain.

Mikis didn't understand. What had he done wrong? He kneeled down and crawled into the new stable to see if anything about it felt strange. He tried to see the stable through a donkey's eyes. Was the step too high? Did the windows let in too much light? Did the new wood smell funny?

Mikis decided to try one last time during Christmas vacation. He and Elena hung old sheets over the windows and put Tsaki's old, familiar feeding trough in her new stable. He spread some extra straw. He filled the rack with hay and fetched Tsaki. But even then Tsaki still refused to take a step inside.

"Suit yourself," said Mikis, and he took Tsaki back to her musty, drafty, damp old stable. There was nothing else he could do.

"Pappou," said Mikis at the end of that miserable day, "I give up."

"You did your best, my boy," said Grandpa.

Mikis asked Grandpa if he understood why Tsaki would

rather stay in her dark old stable than in her light and bright new home.

Grandpa took a deep breath and pulled Mikis onto his lap. He hadn't done that for a while. "Look, it's like this," said Grandpa. "Animals don't like change. And Tsaki's nice and comfortable in her old stable. It's her home."

Grandma came and sat with them and she nodded. "I used to have a little bird," she said. "A canary. I kept it in a cage and one day, after feeding it, I forgot to close the door."

"Did it fly away?" asked Mikis.

"Well, that's the thing," said Grandma. "The next day it was still sitting there inside its cage."

"So what did you do?"

"I decided that I'd never close the cage door again."

25

It was just after Christmas break and the children were sitting together in their circle in the classroom. Miss Chrysi's hair wasn't flat, but was bouncing in curls around her face.

"Is it too cold for the motorbike?" asked Nitsa.

Miss Chrysi said it wasn't.

The class fell silent. No one wanted to talk about what they'd done during Christmas vacation anymore. It was obvious that something was up with Miss Chrysi.

"Tell us what's wrong, Miss," said Anna.

She shook her head and asked if anyone had done anything that they wanted to talk about.

No, no one had any stories to tell. They all looked at Miss Chrysi, because she clearly had some news, but she didn't seem to want to tell anyone.

"Is the motorbike broken?" asked Andreas.

"Something like that," said Miss Chrysi. She didn't really have to explain, because the children already understood.

In the winter, there wasn't as much work for Tsaki to do, so Mikis sometimes took her out after school. Peppi had moved into the stable in Kostas's yard for the colder months, so Mikis and Tsaki went for a walk around the village instead of going to visit him.

When they walked by, everyone said, "Has she moved

into her new stable?" And Mikis called back to them, "No, not yet!" But he was sure that one day she would step through the door all by herself, without a rope, without a blindfold, and without her old stable being demolished.

Every day, Grandma and Grandpa burned the wood that Tsaki had carried down the mountain the previous summer. The huge stack grew smaller and smaller. "By the time the wood's all gone," said Grandpa, "winter will already be over." But it kept on raining and it stayed cold.

"Before long, it'll be warmer in Tsaki's stable than it is in here," said Grandma.

Mikis thought it would be a good idea if they all went to live with Tsaki when they ran out of wood. Then she wouldn't be on her own anymore. And Miss Chrysi could come join them and so could Peppi, and they could all keep one another happy and warm until spring.

When the sun finally reappeared, Grandpa went to work in the olive grove, chopping down trees and gathering wood so that he could stock up for next winter.

"It's about time Tsaki went back to work," Grandpa said to Mikis one day. "Have you seen that tummy of hers? If she gets any bigger, I won't be able to fasten the strap for the baskets. A tractor can stand still for a while, but a donkey has to keep on moving."

Mikis sighed and said, "Pappou, how many times do I have to tell you? Tsaki is not a tractor."

"I know, my boy, I know," said Grandpa. "Tsaki is a donkey. She's a donkey and she has feelings."

26

One morning, when Mikis was at home eating his breakfast, Grandpa suddenly appeared in the kitchen. Mom wasn't even dressed yet and Dad was still shaving upstairs.

"Come with me," Grandpa said to Mikis.

"The boy has to go to school," said Mom.

"He has to come with me."

"No! No way!" said Mom. "Since you've had that donkey he hardly spends any time at home, and now you want to keep him away from school too? He's not going with you. And that's final!"

"Who's there?" asked Dad from the bathroom.

"It's Babas," said Mom, "and he wants to take Mikis with him."

Dad came dashing downstairs. Half of his face was still covered with white shaving foam. "What's going on?" he said.

Mikis looked at his mom, then his dad. He'd never heard his parents talk to Grandpa like that before.

"But . . ." said Grandpa.

"That boy is going to school and if that donkey of yours is being stubborn you'll just have to sort it out by yourself."

Mikis didn't know whether to listen to Dad or Grandpa.

"But Tsaki . . ." said Grandpa.

Mikis couldn't take it any longer. He jumped up, pulled

Grandpa outside, and asked him what was wrong with Tsaki. His heart was thumping against his ribs. He didn't care about school if Tsaki was in trouble. He was Mikis the donkey boy and he had to do whatever he could to help his friend.

Grandpa started his scooter. They raced across the village square, left, right, along the alleyways, up and up, past the house with a thousand flowers, around the corner, into the yard, into the stable and . . .

"Shh," said Grandpa.

It was so dark inside the stable that Mikis could hardly see anything at first. "Tsaki," he said quietly. "Tsaki, are you there?" Then he felt a soft nose against his cheek. When his eyes became used to the darkness he saw that Tsaki wasn't alone. There was a tiny little creature beside her in the straw . . . a donkey foal!

Then Dad stormed into the stable. His shirt was buttoned up wrong and his hair was still all a mess.

"Hand over my boy!" he said to Grandpa.

Grandpa turned around and said, "Son, you really need to be quiet for a moment."

That did the trick. And when Dad saw what had happened, he put his hand over his mouth and he said nothing at all for a long time.

Mikis stroked the foal's furry back. He'd never felt anything that soft before.

"I think," Grandpa whispered to Mikis, "that you know who the foal's father is, don't you?"

27

The morning meeting was long over by the time Mikis came racing into the classroom. He didn't notice that everyone was busily working away in silence, he didn't notice that Andreas was suddenly sitting next to Elena, he didn't notice that Miss Chrysi's hair was flat on her head and there wasn't a single curl in sight. He ran up to the front of the class and stood in front of the blackboard and shouted, "Tsaki had a baby! She's a mom!"

All of the children stopped doing their math lesson. Miss Chrysi asked what was going on. And when Mikis had finished telling the story, she smiled and said quietly, "This spring is off to such a wonderful start."

"Can I come with you this afternoon?" Elena whispered when Mikis sat down behind her.

"Of course," said Mikis. "You have to come." And then he noticed where Andreas was sitting. "Have you moved?" Mikis asked him.

"Someone had to help me with my math problems," said Andreas. Elena nodded.

Mikis took out his math book but he couldn't concentrate, because his head was full of Tsaki. He tapped Elena on the back. "Do you think Peppi . . . ?" he began.

Elena kept her lips tightly shut.

"What? Is Peppi the father?" said Andreas. He was trying

to whisper, but it came out really loud.

Mikis shrugged to say he had no idea.

Miss Chrysi told them to be quiet.

Have you noticed anything about Miss Chrysi? said the note that Andreas passed to Mikis a little later. Mikis looked at Miss Chrysi and realized that she'd been wearing her helmet again. "Looks like the motorbike's fixed," whispered Andreas.

Then Miss Chrysi suddenly appeared beside Andreas and Mikis. She stood there with her hands on her hips. "Andreas Anamatidis," she said. "Go back to your own seat."

Andreas picked up his things and went and sat in his usual place next to Mikis.

When Miss Chrysi was back at her desk, Mikis wrote a note to Elena: *Do you think Peppi's the dad?* He threw it onto Elena's desk. After she'd read it, she gave a quick nod.

Mikis wrote her another note: *But when?*

Elena turned around. "Don't you get it?" she said. And then Mikis realized. Elena had said that Tsaki and Peppi were getting along really, really well that first day in the olive grove. He'd made her shake hands and promise not to say anything about what had happened, and that was exactly what she'd done. After all, a promise is a promise.

28

It was absolute chaos in the classroom that day. No one could concentrate at all. Everyone was too busy talking about Miss Chrysi's hair and Tsaki's foal. After lunch, Miss Chrysi said, "This is a very special day. It's a red-letter day." The class stayed silent as everyone wondered what exactly a red-letter day was.

"A foal has been born," she continued, her eyes looking a little watery, "and um . . . well, what I wanted to say is . . ."

"The motorbike's fixed," said Andreas.

Miss Chrysi looked in surprise at Andreas. "How did you know?" All of the children pointed at her hair. And Miss Chrysi started to laugh. And she laughed so much that she nearly fell off her chair! Spiros stood up and did a little dance. Anna joined in, and Nitsa, and then the whole class. Everyone was dancing away. And Mikis and Elena were the happiest dancers of all — because they knew that Tsaki was never going to be lonely again.

After school, Mikis ran with Elena and Andreas to Grandma and Grandpa's house. They flew over the village square, through the narrow alleyways, left, right, up and up, past the house with a thousand flowers, around the corner, past the giant cactus, and into the yard, where Grandpa was stacking the wood for next winter.

"You're so late!" cried Grandpa.

"Late?" said Mikis. "We couldn't have got here any faster!"

Grandpa told them to come with him and he strode over to the new stable, where Tsaki was gazing out through the open top half of the door and munching happily away.

"Pappou!" cried Mikis.

"Yes, it's a miracle," said Grandpa.

He told them that he had picked up the little foal and carried it from the old stable to the new one.

"And then what? What happened next?" said Andreas.

"What happened next," said Grandpa, "was that Tsaki just followed me, as if it was the most natural thing in the world."

Mikis jumped up and threw his arms around Grandpa's neck. Elena jumped up after him. If Grandpa could carry a donkey, he could certainly lift two children. As he put them back down, he said, "And now you've got to come up with a name for the foal. It's a girl." And he gave Mikis a wink.

29

Mikis, Elena, and Andreas climbed over the door into Tsaki's new stable. The baby foal was very small. It was a mini-donkey, almost small enough to sit on your lap.

"Listen carefully, Tsaki," said Mikis. "You know how this works now, so pay attention." He explained to Andreas and Elena what they were going to do.

"So we're looking for a girl's name," said Mikis.

"Something like Sissi?" said Elena.

Tsaki blinked her eyes.

"Something like that," said Mikis. And they took turns to suggest a long list of names.

"Athene," said Mikis.

"Ariadne," said Elena.

"Chrysi," said Andreas.

"Medusa," said Mikis.

"Nausicaa," said Elena.

"Papadakis," said Andreas.

"But that's the doctor's name," said Elena.

"So what?" said Andreas.

"Kriti," said Mikis.

"Sirene," said Elena.

"Andreas," said Andreas.

Tsaki didn't react. She just stared outside and went on calmly chewing her hay.

"Aliki," they continued. "Irini, Anna, Nana, Maria, Zita, Evi."

"Sissi," said Elena again.

And what do you think Tsaki did? She gave a great big blink!

Athene   Ariadne   Chrysi   Medusa

Nausicaa   Papadakis   Kriti   Sirene

Andreas   Aliki   Irini   Anna

Nana   Maria   Zita   Evi

Sissi

AFTERWORD

In the summer of 2009, I was invited to stay in a house on the island of Corfu for two weeks to write a story about donkeys. I didn't know anything about donkeys at the time. Nothing at all. But I did know that there was a donkey sanctuary on Corfu. So I went for a visit. The sanctuary was full of old donkeys. Some of them were lame. Others had bad backs from carrying heavy baskets. One donkey was blind.

I took a rope and Aviro, the blind donkey, let me tie it to his halter. Then we went for a very slow walk along the narrow roads near the donkey sanctuary. Three dogs who lived there came along for the walk. I didn't need to tell Aviro where the tasty grass was, because he sniffed it out for himself.

The woman who runs the donkey sanctuary is called Judy. She works with volunteers to take care of retired working donkeys, which are often sick and injured when they are brought in. Some of the donkeys end up in the Netherlands, where I live, at the donkey sanctuary in the town of Zeist.

Tsaki was one of the first donkeys at the donkey sanctuary on Corfu. And that's why the donkey in this book is called Tsaki, as a very small tribute to every working donkey, all over the world.

— Bibi

BIBI DUMON TAK is a Dutch author who has written a number of books for young readers, including *Soldier Bear* (Eerdmans), which won the 2012 Mildred L. Batchelder Award. She was inspired to write this story after visiting a donkey sanctuary on the Greek island of Corfu.

PHILIP HOPMAN studied at the Rietveld Academy in Amsterdam and has illustrated more than 150 books, including *Earth to Stella* (Clarion), *22 Orphans* (Kane/Miller), and *Soldier Bear* (Eerdmans). He lives in the Netherlands.

LAURA WATKINSON translates from Dutch, Italian, and German, and has a special interest in books for younger readers. Her translation of Bibi Dumon Tak's *Soldier Bear* won the 2012 Batchelder Award. She lives in Amsterdam.